Go! Go! Dino!

Written and Illustrated by
Kaz Windness

Ready-to-Read

Simon Spotlight

New York London Toronto Sydney New Delhi

T0338377

SIMON SPOTLIGHT
An imprint of Simon & Schuster Children's Publishing Division
1230 Avenue of the Americas, New York, New York 10020
This Simon Spotlight edition May 2024
All rights reserved, including the right of reproduction in whole or in part in any form.
SIMON SPOTLIGHT, READY-TO-READ, and colophon are registered
trademarks of Simon & Schuster, LLC.
Simon & Schuster: Celebrating 100 Years of Publishing in 2024
For information about special discounts for bulk purchases, please contact
Simon & Schuster Special Sales at 1-866-506-1949 or business@simonandschuster.com.
The Simon & Schuster Speakers Bureau can bring authors to your live event.
For more information or to book an event contact the Simon & Schuster Speakers Bureau
at 1-866-248-3049 or visit our website at www.simonspeakers.com.
Manufactured in the United States of America 0324 LAK
2 4 6 8 10 9 7 5 3 1
This book has been cataloged with the Library of Congress.
ISBN 978-1-6659-4427-4 (hc)
ISBN 978-1-6659-4426-7 (pbk)
ISBN 978-1-6659-4428-1 (ebook)

For Alec. You're go,
go, going places!
—K. W.

Banners waving,
spotlights glowing.
Where are all the dinos going?

When you hear the whistle blow . . .

Dino racers, GO! GO! GO!

Pump your pedals!
Roll and slide!
Down the track,
the dinos glide.

Brontosaurus slow to start,
munching, crunching
at the cart.

Stegosaurus gaining speed.

T. rex thunders to the lead!

Brontosaurus full and happy, takes a little dino nappy.

Pedals pumping!
Weaving . . .
jumping!

Uh-oh, dinos! Tires bumping!

Watch out, dinos!
STOP! STOP! STOP!

T. rex wrecks Triceratops!

Dinos pile up
on the track.
Stegosaurus
skirts the stack.

Dinos howl and dinos stamp.
Stegosaurus is our champ!

Flags are waving!
Horns are blowing!
Why is Stegosaurus slowing?

"First is such a lonely place,
without friends
to share the race."

Stegosaurus turns around,
picking dinos off the ground.

"Leave behind your bikes and skates. You can ride between my plates!"

Dino fans let out a ROAR
so loud it wakes a dinosaur.

Skating at a
lightning pace,
Brontosaurus
joins the race.

Stegosaurus does not worry.
"We will win.
No need to hurry."
Brontosaurus is
much slower . . .

. . . but she has
a neck to lower!

A tie! A tie! All dinos win!